The Boxer and the Princess

written and illustrated by HELME HEINE

translated from the German

Margaret K. McElderry Books

Max was different from the other young rhinoceroses.
He was gentle and sensitive.
"Life is hard," said his father. "You must learn to stand up for yourself,
and most of all, you need a thick skin!"
Max nodded obediently.

Mosquitoes pestered him from morning till late at night
because he tasted so sweet.
So he traded his pony
for a pair of boxing gloves.
Then he had peace.

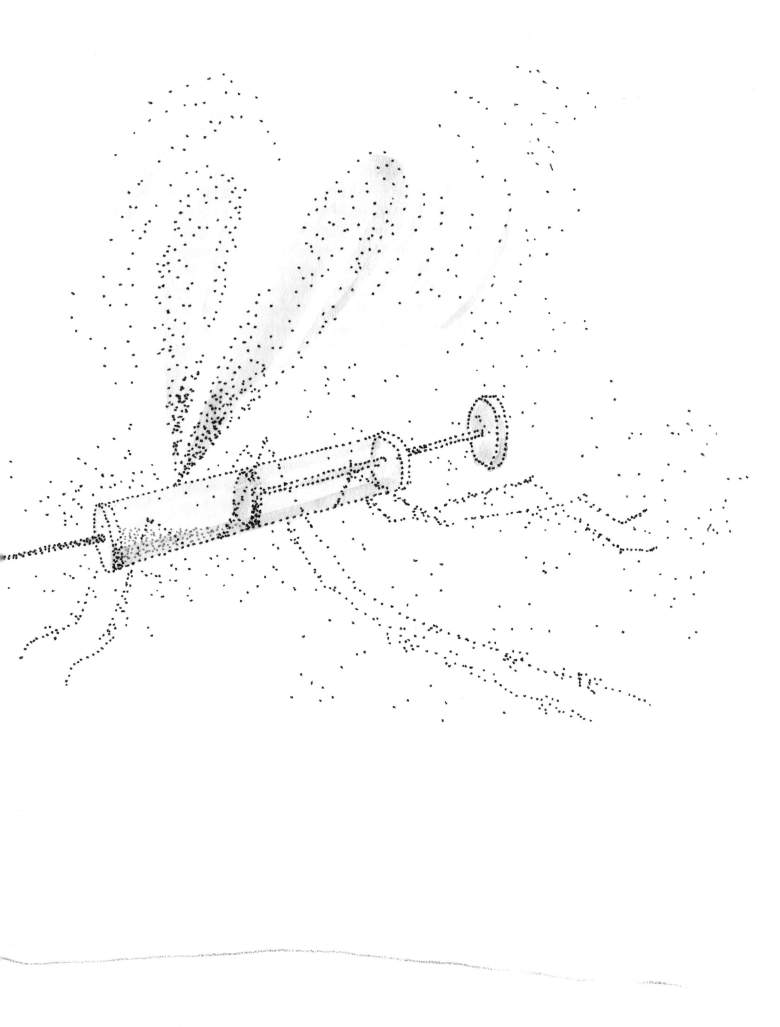

The soles of Max's feet were so tender
that even stepping on an ant hurt him.
So he got some army boots.
Then he could wander around safely.

Max's skin was so thin
that when he and his friends raided the cherry orchard
he was always the first one caught.
The farmer could see right through him!
So he got a suit of armor made of iron.
Then the cherries could not be seen.

Max's horn was so delicate that it bent over
when a butterfly rested on it.
So he popped a knight's iron helmet over his head.
Then he had the thickest skin on earth.

Now Max thought that he was strong and grown-up. Lions would find him a tough nut to crack, and wasps would bend their stingers on him. He was shielded all around. Only cold and loneliness found a way through his armor.

From then on, Max did whatever pleased him!
He went to sleep when it suited him.

He never had to use soap.
He sometimes answered back—or not at all.

And when his father gave him a spanking,
it didn't bother Max one bit, only his father!
His parents did not know what to do.

Even the doctor could not help, although he x-rayed Max from every angle.
Max and all his feelings were locked up tight, and there was no key to open him.

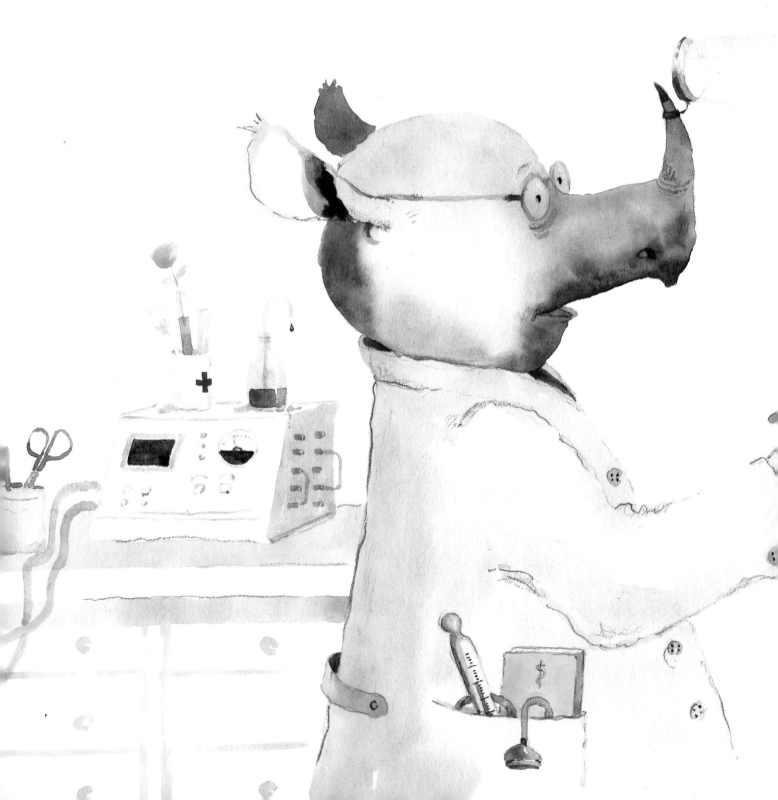

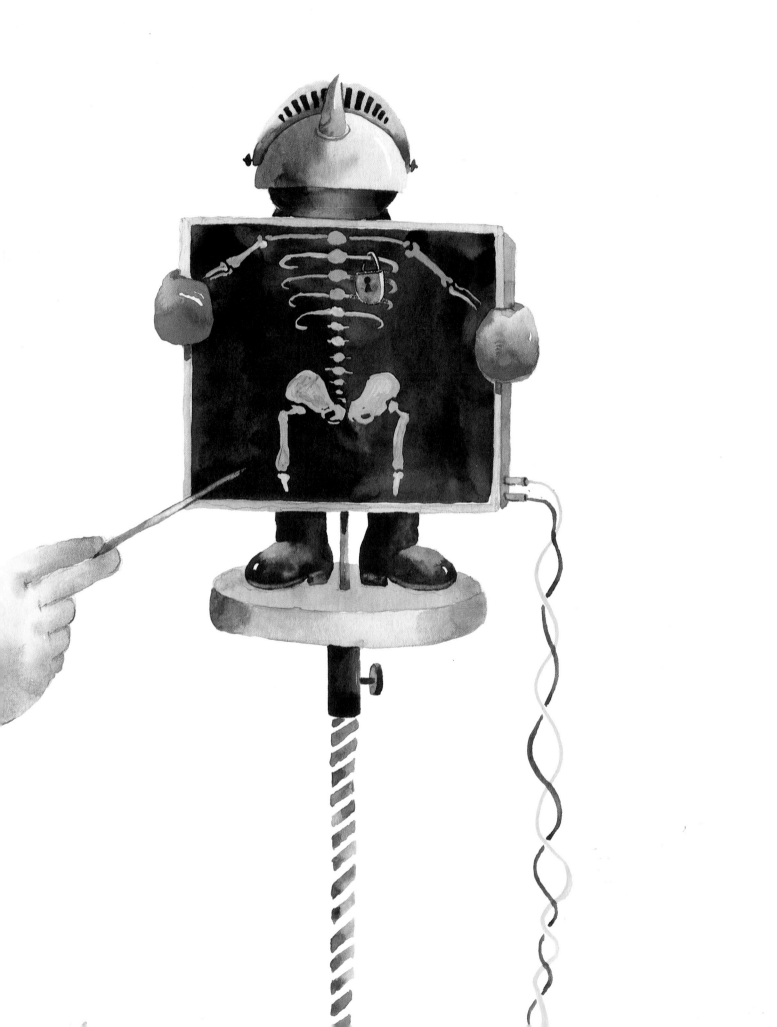

His parents decided to let him travel wherever
he wanted, to see the world.
"Be sure you eat enough and go to bed early,"
his mother cried, "and send us a postcard."
"And don't forget," rumbled his father,
"we'll always be around when you need us."

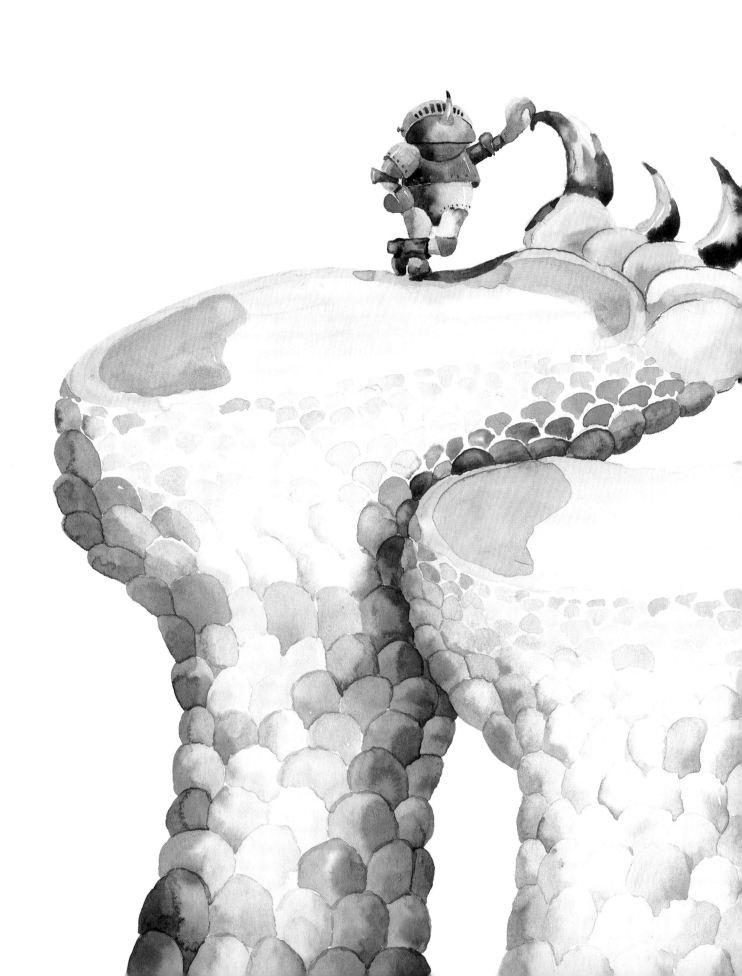

Max became a splendid knight.
He never hid from a single dragon.
No matter how big or how strong the dragons were,
he defeated them all.

One day he rescued a princess who was in chains.
She was beautiful, and he asked her to marry him.
But the princess refused to marry a boxer.

So Max took off his boxing gloves and picked her some flowers.
He wanted to walk the tightrope with the princess.
So he got rid of his boots to get a better grip with his feet.

When they went swimming, he unlocked his armor.
Then the princess could see his heart.

After their swim, they kissed, and it was much nicer without the helmet.

Each kiss made Max stronger than ten suits of armor.

So Max and the princess got married.
They lived happily ever after in a palace made of glass,

and Max became the favorite king of all the rhinoceroses.

His suit of armor stands in their garden – just in case of need.

Margaret K. McElderry Books
An imprint of Simon & Schuster Children's Publishing Division
1230 Avenue of the Americas
New York, NY 10020

The text of this book is set in Aldus
The illustrations were rendered in watercolors.
Printed in Italy

10 9 8 7 6 5 4 3 2 1

ISBN 0-689-82195-6
Library of Congress Catalog Card Number: 97-76298